This Little Tiger
book belongs to:

_____

_____

_____

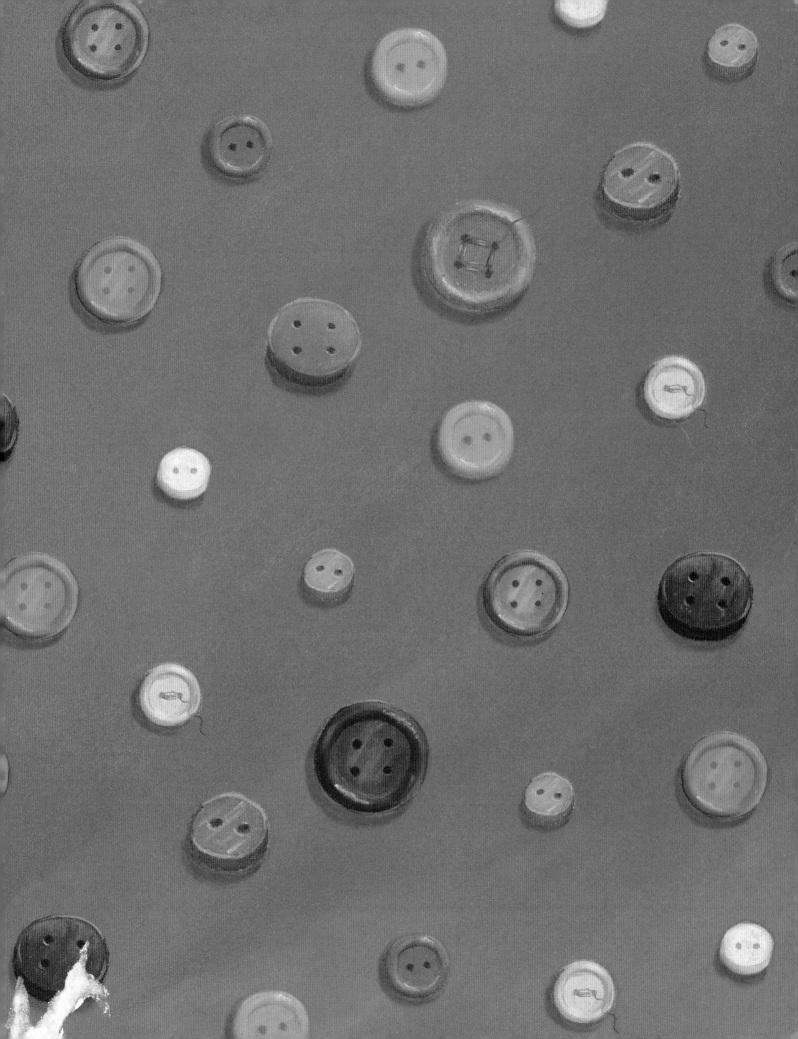

For Maya and Leila, with love
~ M C B

For Lara M Bahrani
~ T M

LITTLE TIGER PRESS
1 The Coda Centre,
189 Munster Road, London SW6 6AW
www.littletiger.co.uk
First published in Great Britain 2014
This edition published 2015
Text copyright © M Christina Butler 2014
Illustrations copyright © Tina Macnaughton 2014

M Christina Butler and Tina Macnaughton have asserted
their rights to be identified as the author and illustrator of this
work under the Copyright, Designs and Patents Act, 1988

One Special Sleepover

M Christina Butler   •   Tina Macnaughton

LITTLE TIGER PRESS
London

Little Hedgehog was bustling round his
brand new tree house. He was having his
first ever sleepover and he couldn't wait
for his friends to arrive.

"Anyone at home?" called Badger.

"Come on up!" laughed
Little Hedgehog excitedly.

"Oh, this is lovely!" Rabbit gasped as the friends climbed up.

"We brought you a present!" said Mouse. "It's a book of bedtime stories."

"Thank you," smiled Little Hedgehog. "And I've got a present for you. Look!"

Brilliant Bedtime Stories

"Taa-daah!" cheered Little Hedgehog,
pulling out a colourful, cosy blanket.
"I made it specially! And it's big enough
for all of us to snuggle under."

But as Little Hedgehog shook
out the blanket, a gust of wind
blew it up into the air and
over the treetops!

"Oh no!" cried
Little Hedgehog.

"Quick!" yelled Fox,
scrambling down the
ladder. "Follow that
blanket!"

"The wind's blowing
it towards the river!"
puffed Badger.

But by the time they reached the riverbank the blanket had flopped into the water and was floating away.

"What are we going to do?" sniffed
Little Hedgehog. "We can't have
a sleepover without a blanket!"
"Don't be sad," said Badger.
"Why don't we try and make
a new one?"
"That's a wonderful idea,
Badger!" smiled Little Hedgehog.

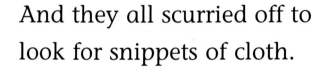

And they all scurried off to look for snippets of cloth.

"Look, Little Hedgehog!" said Badger as the friends shared the things they'd found. "You slept on this cushion cover after the Big Storm blew your house away."

"Oh yes, I remember," sighed Little Hedgehog. "You were so kind, and I was so cosy and warm in front of your fire."

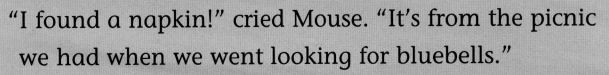

"I found a napkin!" cried Mouse. "It's from the picnic we had when we went looking for bluebells."

"Poor Mouse!" said Little Hedgehog, shaking his head. "That was the day you fell down that deep, dark hole."

"I know," giggled Mouse. "I'd still be there if you hadn't pulled me out!"

"Can this go in our blanket?" squeaked
a baby mouse, snuggling into a piece
of cloth covered with stars.

"Of course," smiled Little Hedgehog.
"Does it remind you of anything?"

"Yes!" cried the babies. "When we went to
watch the shooting stars!"

"That was such a special night," added
Mouse as the friends snipped, sewed and
shared their stories together.

In no time at all the blanket was finished.

"Every patch and stitch will remind us of the happy times we've spent together," said Little Hedgehog. "Let's call it our Friendship Blanket!"

"What a lovely idea!" said Badger. "That's just what it is, and we've all helped to make it."

"Hurrah!" they cheered, shaking out their wonderful blanket.
  But Rabbit gasped as a baby mouse peeped through a hole in the middle. "Oh dear! We need more cloth!"

"But I've got nothing left!"
cried Little Hedgehog sadly.
"I used all my material to
make the first blanket!"

Suddenly, the two little birds
flew in carrying a piece of
bright red cloth.

"It's from your lost blanket,
Little Hedgehog!" cried Fox.
"They must have found it
near the river."

"Oh, thank you!" called
Little Hedgehog. "It'll fit
perfectly."

Little Hedgehog's needle flashed
in the lantern light as he stitched
the very last square into place.

"Now there's a patchwork piece
from all of us!" he cried and all
his friends cheered.

The woods grew dark and the tree house swayed gently in the night wind. Everyone snuggled beneath the blanket as Badger read a story.

"All my friends together," Little Hedgehog whispered happily. "What a perfect sleepover!"

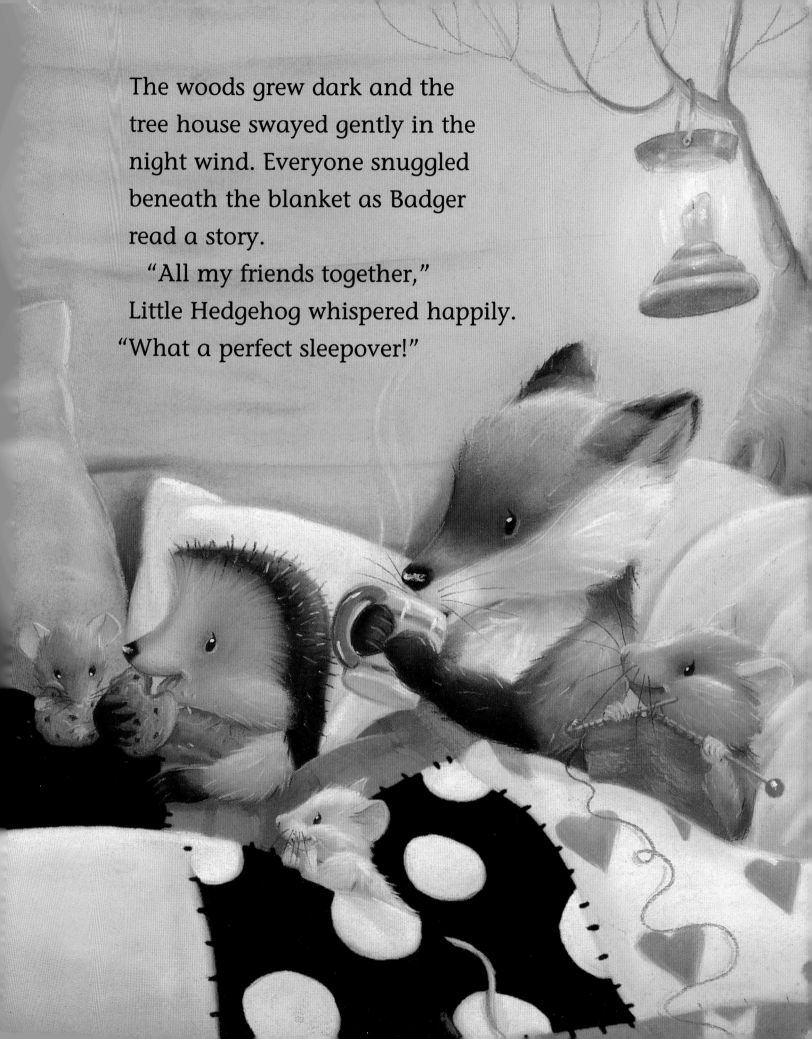

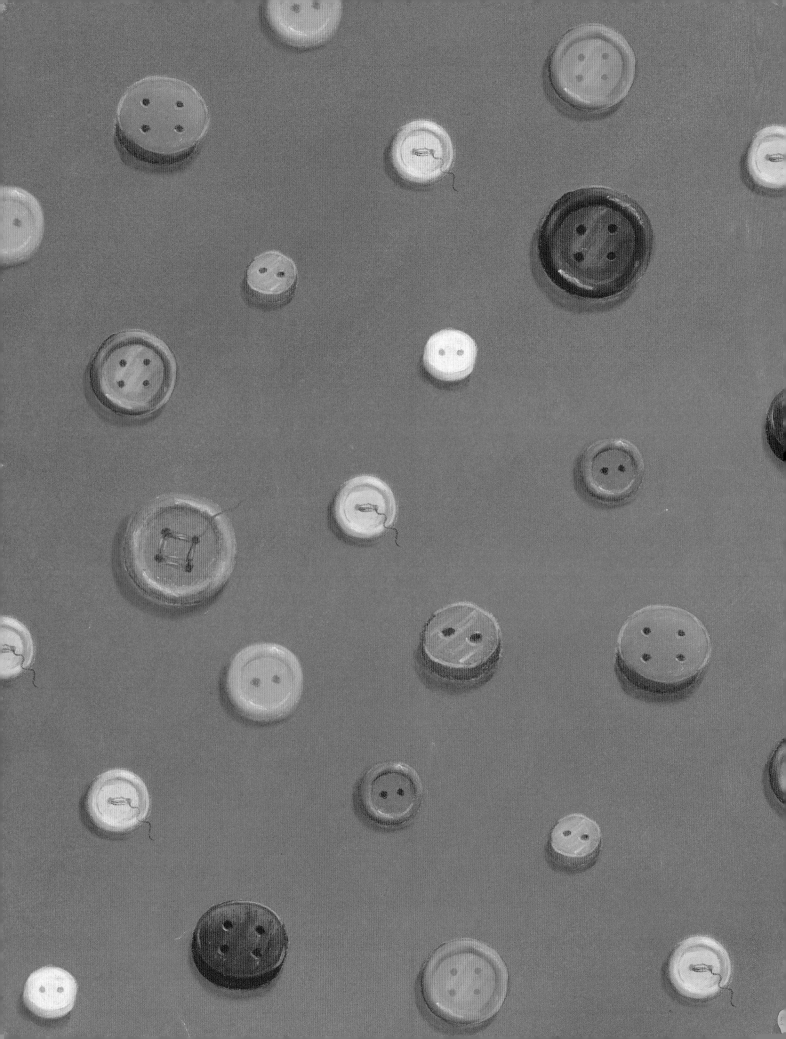

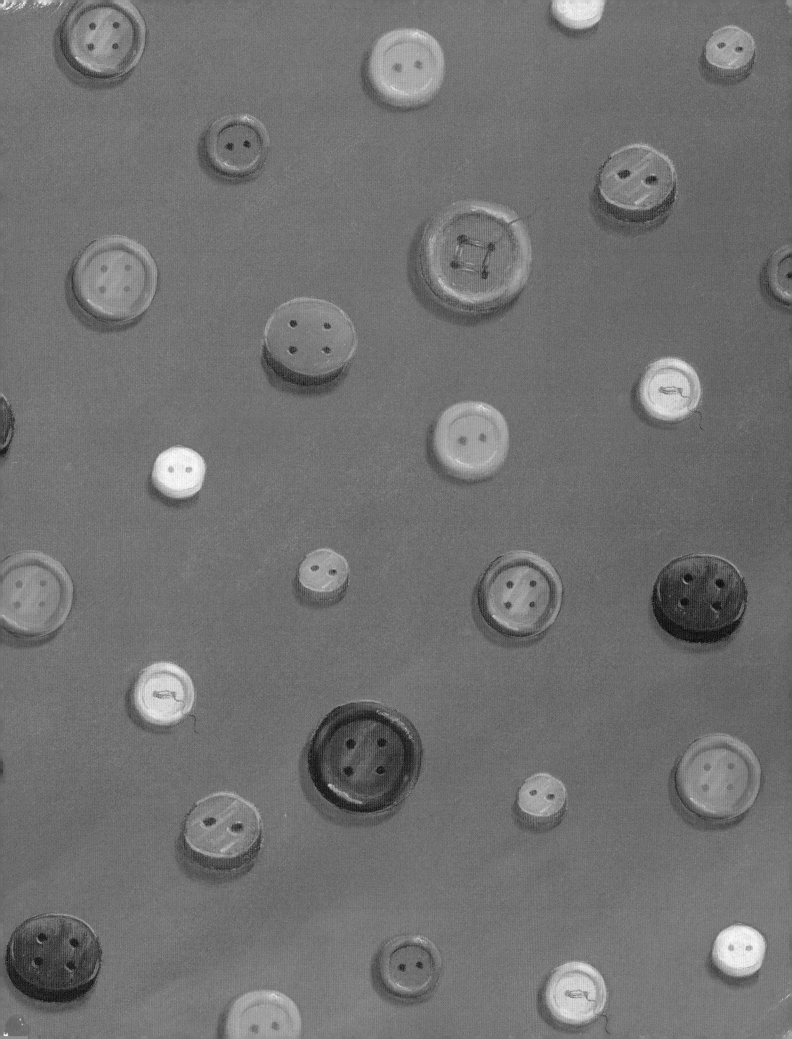

If you like the *Little Hedgehog* stories, you'll love these books!

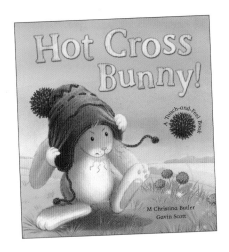

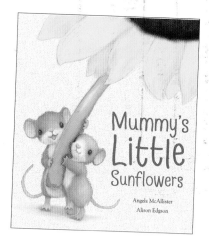

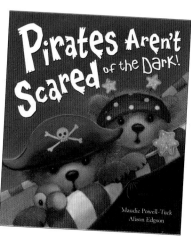

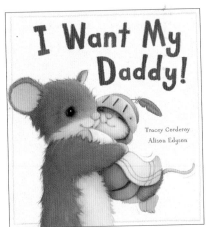

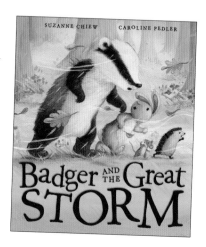

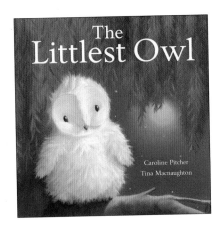

For information regarding any of the above titles or for our catalogue, please contact us:
Little Tiger Press, 1 The Coda Centre,
189 Munster Road, London SW6 6AW
Tel: 020 7385 6333
E-mail: contact@littletiger.co.uk
www.littletiger.co.uk